WHITE SNOW
BRIGHT SNOW

WHITE SNOW BRIGHT SNOW

By Alvin Tresselt

Illustrated by Roger Duvoisin

Lothrop, Lee & Shepard Books
New York

Library of Congress Cataloging in Publication Data
Tresselt, Alvin R. White snow, bright snow.
   Summary: When it begins to look, feel, and smell like snow, everyone prepares for a winter
blizzard.   [1. Snow—Fiction.]   I. Duvoisin, Roger, 1900-1980   ill.
II. Title. PZ7.T732Wh   1989   [E]   88-45871
ISBN 0-688-41161-4   ISBN 0-688-51161-9 (lib. bdg.)

Softly, gently in the secret night,

Down from the North came the quiet white.

Drifting, sifting, silent flight,

Softly, gently, in the secret night.

●

White snow, bright snow, smooth and deep.

Light snow, night snow, quiet as sleep.

Down, down, without a sound;

Down, down, to the frozen ground.

●

Covering roads and hiding fences,

Sifting in cracks and filling up trenches.

Millions of snowflakes, tiny and light,

Softly, gently, in the secret night.

The postman
said it looked
like snow.
The farmer
said it smelled
like snow.

The policeman said it felt
like snow, and his wife said
her big toe hurt, and
that always meant snow.

Even the rabbits knew it, and scurried around

in the dead leaves.

While the children watched the low grey sky,

waiting for the first snowflake to fall.

Then, just when no one was looking, it came.

One flake, two flakes, five, eight, ten, and suddenly

the air was filled with soft powdery snowflakes,

whispering quietly as they sifted down.

The postman

put on his rubbers.

The farmer

went to the barn

for a snow shovel.

The policeman buttoned up
his coat. His wife made sure she
had cough mixture
in the medicine cabinet.

But the children laughed and danced, trying to catch the lacy snowflakes on their tongues.

While the rabbits hid in their warm burrows under the ground.

Faster and faster came the tiny snowflakes, and the brown earth turned white.

Fields and stone walls, roads and gutters, lawns and side-walks, all were buried under the soft white snow. It covered the roofs of houses, and piled on top of chimneys. It filled the cold tree branches with great white blossoms. And when night came, icy cold snowflakes sparkled in the light of the street lamps.

The postman

slipped and fell into a snowbank.

The farmer

dug a path from

his house

to the barn.

The policeman got his
feet wet, and had to
soak them in a tub of
hot water.

His wife put a mustard
plaster on his chest so he
wouldn't catch cold.

The rabbits stirred in their sleep, deep in their warm burrows under the ground, under the snow.

And the children dreamed of snow houses and snow-men as they slept in their snug beds under the roof-tops, under the snow.

Silently, the frost made pictures of ice ferns on the window panes.

Then without a sound, just when everybody was asleep, the snow stopped, and bright stars filled the night.

★　　★　　★

In the morning a clear blue sky was overhead and blue shadows hid in all the corners.

Automobiles looked like big fat raisins buried in snowdrifts.

Houses crouched together, their windows peeking out from under great white eyebrows.

Even the church steeple wore a pointed cap on its top.

The postman put
away his rubbers and took out
his high boots.
The farmer milked his cows
in a barn filled with
bright snow-light.

The policeman

had a chill,

and stayed in bed.

His wife sat in a rocker

and knitted a long woolen

scarf for him.

The rabbits hopped about as best they could,
making long funny rabbit tracks in the soft snow.
The children made a snowman, a snow house,
a snow fort, and then had a snowball fight.

The wind pushed light puffs of white from the
branches, while the melting snow on roof-tops
drip-drip-dripped into long shiny icicles.
Each day the sun grew stronger, and the snow melted.
Big patches of soft muddy ground showed
through the snow in the fields.
The sound of dripping, running water and the smell
of wet brown earth filled the warm air.
Now the branches were bare again and grey pussy
willows pushed out of their brown shells.
Fence posts lost their dunce caps, the snowman's
arms dropped off, and running water gurgled
in gutters and rain pipes.

The postman slowly delivered his mail so he could enjoy the bright sunshine. The farmer let his cows out in the barnyard for the first time since winter began.

The policeman's cold
was better, and he swung
his club in the air as he
walked in the park.

His wife dug around
under the lilac bush,
looking for the
snowdrops and crocuses
that grew there.
While the rabbits spent
all their time hopping
about in the warm
world above the ground.

And the children watched

for the first robin to tell them

Spring had really come.

ABOUT WHITE SNOW, BRIGHT SNOW

Alvin Tresselt writes: "*White Snow, Bright Snow* had its beginning as I walked a street in New York City on a snowy winter night. The poem came first, and the verses all but wrote themselves in my head as I walked along. When it came to the story, I recalled my mother saying that her big toe always hurt whenever it was going to snow. This brought to mind the ways other people could tell it was going to snow, and I applied these to my cast of characters: the farmer, the postman, the policeman, and of course his practical-minded wife. And what would snow be without children to enjoy it! After that the story unfolded with very little difficulty. But seasons, like stories, come to an end, so what better way to end the story than to have the children watch for the first robin to tell them that winter was over, and spring was once more on the way."

Alvin Tresselt and Roger Duvoisin were teamed together as author and illustrator on fourteen picture books for very young children that were published by Lothrop, Lee & Shepard Books. *White Snow, Bright Snow* was their first collaboration. Alvin Tresselt grew up in Passaic, New Jersey, and worked in children's book publishing in New York City for many years. Roger Duvoisin was born in Geneva, Switzerland, and moved to the United States in 1930. He lived and worked in New York City until 1938, when he became an American citizen and bought land in Gladstone, New Jersey. Tresselt and Duvoisin did not meet until after *White Snow, Bright Snow* was published, yet both brought to the book deep affection for small towns set in the rolling New Jersey countryside.

Roger Duvoisin was awarded the Caldecott Medal in 1948 for his illustrations in *White Snow, Bright Snow.* The Caldecott Medal, named in honor of nineteenth-century English illustrator Randolph Caldecott, is given annually by the Association for Library Service to Children, a division of the American Library Association, to the artist of the most distinguished American picture book for children published in the preceding year.